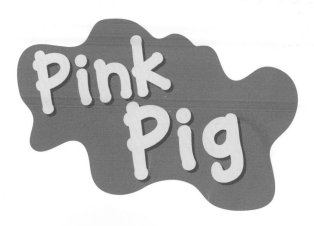

Pink Pig

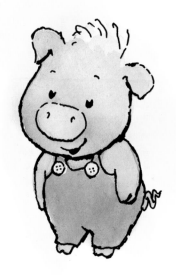

Written by Susan Hayes
Illustrated by Sheila Lucas

Scott Foresman

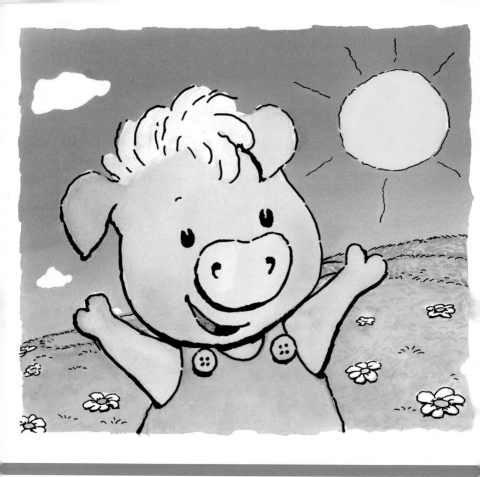

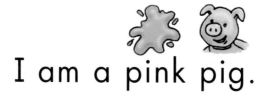

I am a pink pig.

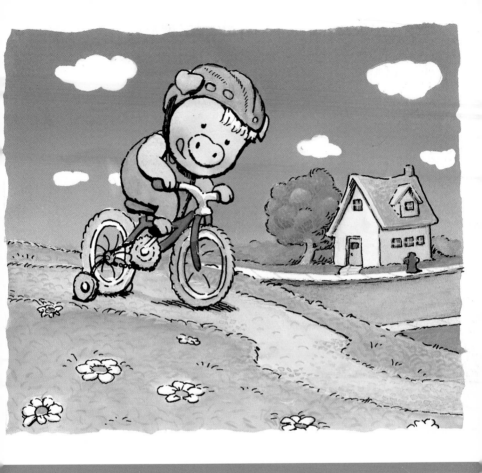

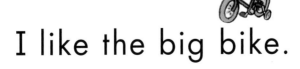
I like the big bike.

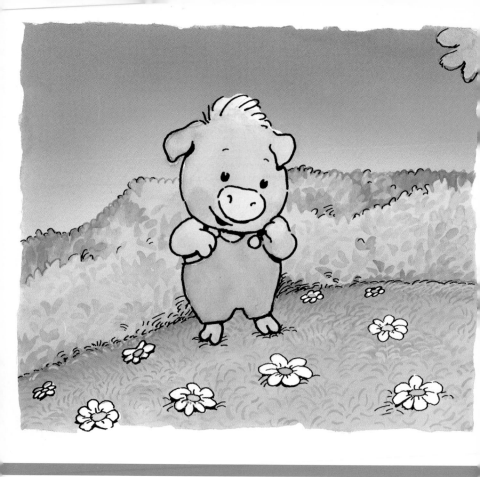

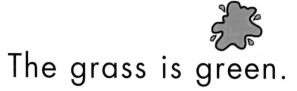

The grass is green.

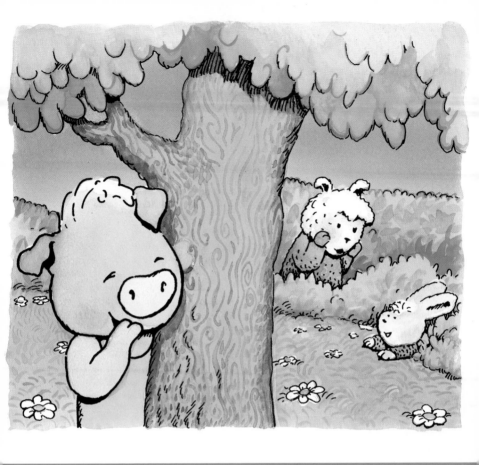

 I am at the big tree.

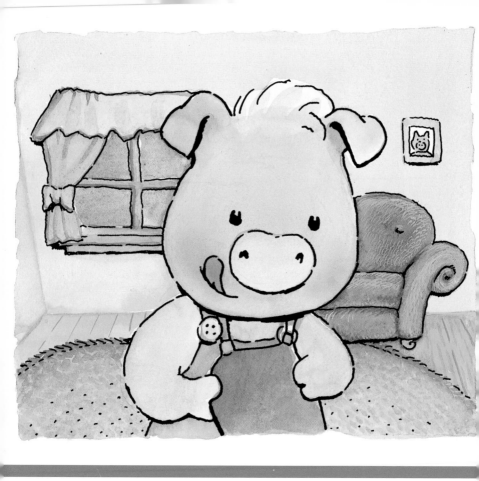

 I am in the house.

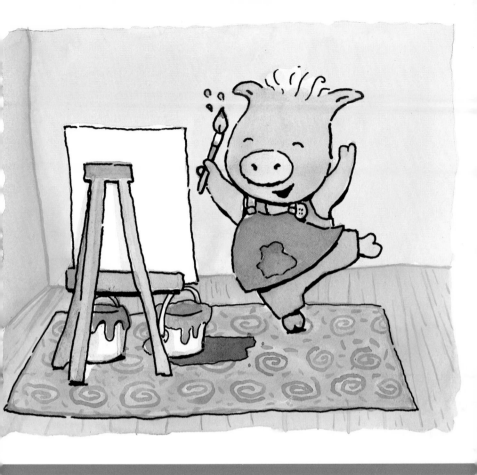

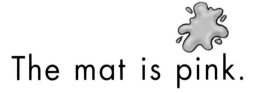 The mat is pink.

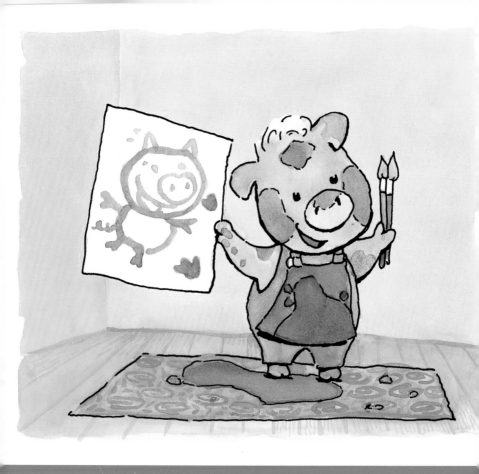

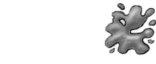

I am a purple pig!